STOMP, CHOMP, BIG ROARS! HERE COME THE DINOSAURS!

by **Kaye Umansky**
Illustrated by **Nick Sharratt**

PUFFIN

STOMP,
CHOMP,
BIG ROARS!

This is the way we stomp our feet,
Stomp! Stomp! Stomp!
This is the way we like to eat,
Chomp! Chomp! Chomp!

Stomp! Chomp! Big roars!
Here come the dinosaurs!

ROAR!

Roar, roar, roar, roar!
I'm a roaring dinosaur!
I may be shy, I may be small,
But I'm the roariest of all.

WALKING TO THE SWAMP

Here we come,
Me and my mum,
Stomp, stomp, STOMP!
We always do it this way
When we're walking
To the swamp.
Let's make
The ground shake,
Stomp, stomp, STOMP!

MAKING FRIENDS

I like to swish my tail like this
And bare my teeth like that.
It shows you that I'm friendly
And would like to have a chat.

I hope you'll swish your tail as well
And bare your teeth at me.
And then we'll be the best of friends
And you can come to tea.

a S h

Six, seven,
Eight, nine, ten,
Time to fill the swamp again!

GRUMPY

Bumpy, bumpy, bumpy,
I'm feeling really grumpy.
I'll stamp my feet and
grind my teeth
To show you all I'm humpy.

THREE LITTLE EGGS

Three little eggs,
Tap, tap, tap!
Out come the babies,
Clap, clap, clap!
Try their tails out,
Flap, flap, flap!
Then settle down
For a nap.
Zzzzzzzzzz.

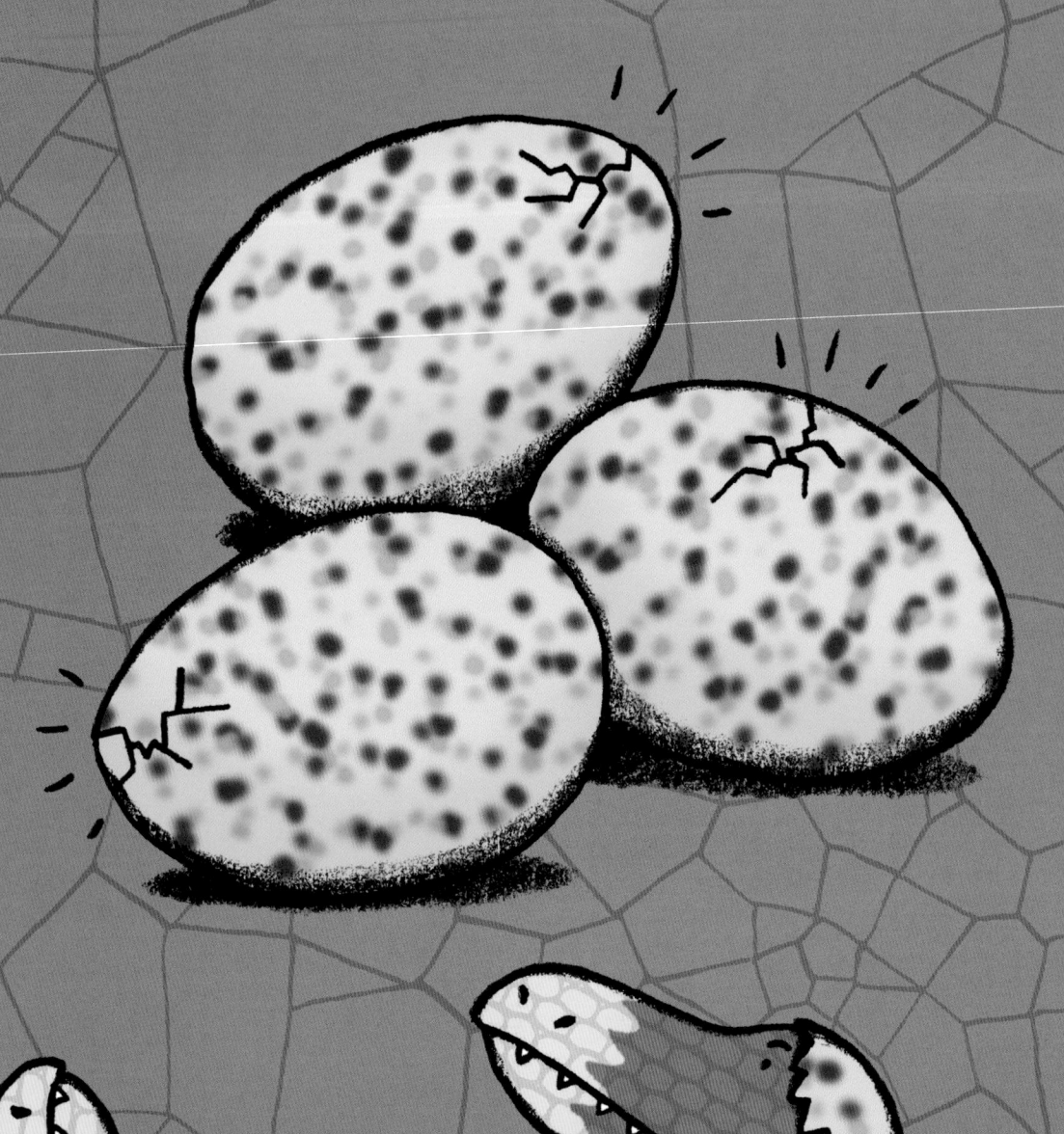

DADDY BIGFOOT

I leave the biggest footprints
When I'm walking in the sand.
But you should see my daddy's,
They're the biggest in the land!

DINOSAUR
FOOD

Dinosaur food, dinosaur food,
I'm in the mood for
Dinosaur food!
Munch, crunch,
Where's lunch?
GIVE ME SOME DINOSAUR FOOD!

ROLY POLY

Roly Poly,
Roly Poly,
Lie down flat
And start off slowly.

Then go faster.
FASTER STILL!
Roly Poly
Down the hill!

Bang, crash!
That was me.
I roly poled
Into a tree!

HIDE AND SEEK

Where are you hiding?
Where can you be?
Deep in a hole?
High in a tree?
Are you near
Or are you far?
I'm looking, I'm looking –
And there you are!

BE A MOUSE

Be a mouse
And walk on tiptoe,
Ever so quiet
With not one sound.

Sssh, sssh,
Creep around,
Ever so quiet
With not one sound.

Be a dinosaur,
Big and noisy!
Stamp your feet
And stomp around!

Stomp! Stomp!
Stomp around!
Stamp your feet
And stomp around!

JUST
SITTING

Sometimes it's nice to stop and sit
And look around a little bit.
To take a rest beneath the sky
And simply watch the world go by.

GOODNIGHT

Dinosaurs get tired too.
Of that there is no doubt.
All that stomping and that roaring
Is enough to wear them out.
Can you see them sleeping?
Can you hear their snores?
See you in the morning.
Goodnight, dinosaurs.

For Richard and Heather - N.S.
For Mo and Ella - K.U.

PUFFIN BOOKS

Published by the Penguin Group: London, New York, Ireland, Australia, Canada, India, New Zealand and South Africa
Penguin Books Ltd, Registered Offices: 80 Strand, London WC2R 0RL, England

puffinbooks.com

Published 2006
015

Text copyright © Kaye Umansky, 2006
Illustrations copyright © Nick Sharratt, 2006

Manufactured in China

ISBN: 978–0–140–56935–3